All I Want For Christmas

For mummy xxx

ORCHARD BOOKS
First published in Great Britain in hardback in 2017 by The Watts Publishing Group
First published in paperback in 2017 • 1 3 5 7 9 10 8 6 4 2 • Text and illustrations © Rachel Bright, 2017
The moral rights of the author have been asserted • All rights reserved
A CIP catalogue record for this book is available from the British Library
HB ISBN 978 1 40833 165 1 • PB ISBN 978 1 40833 166 8
Printed and bound in China

MIX
Paper from
responsible sources
FSC® C104740
FSC
www.fsc.org

Orchard Books • An imprint of Hachette Children's Group • Part of The Watts Publishing Group Limited
Carmelite House, 50 Victoria Embankment, London EC4Y 0DZ
An Hachette UK Company • www.hachette.co.uk • www.hachettechildrens.co.uk

with special thank yous to David

A frosty breeze is blowing
and the snow is on its way.
Every heart is counting down:
it's nearly Christmas Day!

The holidays
are coming.
Yes, they're getting
SUPER near . . .

SUPER CH
ADVENT C

It has to be without a doubt my **FAVOURITE** time of year.

So many things to think of,
so much for us to do . . .

100. Christmas Eve Story
99. Milk + Cookies for Santa
98. Carrot for Ru
97. Tree lights on
96. Lay table
95. Pull crackers
94. Decorate cake
93. Ice cake
92. Peel veg
91. Pu
9

Making, baking, wrapping,

Painting, glittering with glue!

And everyone is thinking
what they'd really like to see,
when they're looking in the morning,

underneath the Christmas tree.

So they write their lists
and write them LONG!
And copy them in case.
Then post them off to Santa . . .

with their
CUTEST
please-please
face!

They're thinking of a brand-new toy or something nice to wear.

A stocking full of naughty treats

or MASSIVE
teddy bear!

But if you ask ME what I want,
the thing I'd really love,
I'd tell you with a
happy heart . . .

it's none of the above!

Yes, when we're getting ready,
together YOU and ME,
when we're hanging up
the sparkles...

on our lovely
Christmas
tree ...

Whilst we're baking
Christmas cookies and
icing up the cake . . .

I'll be thinking
of the thing
I'd like to be there
when I wake . . .

I'll be thinking all about it,
peeling veggies for
the roast.

And when you ask me if I've
put my North pole letter
in the post ...

To Santa
& the Elves
The Grotto
North Pole

a hundred things we must get ready!

Until it's time to go to bed
And snuggle up with teddy . . .

And on the night of Christmas Eve,
we'll have **a** goodnight kiss,

I'll whisper that
there's **nothing**
more I'd ever want
than this . . .

The thing I want
THE WHOLE YEAR ROUND,
The thing I want, it's true . . .
the perfect gift this
Christmas time?

LOVE
FROM
BiG P x

Well that,
my love . . .

But, of course,
p.s. to say . . .

I LOVE my present toOOOOOOO!